KEEP IT 100

Cover image used courtesy of
The Creative Exchange

ISBN: 9781020001260 (Paperback)
ISBN: 9781020001277 (Ebook)

First Edition

Library of Congress Control Number: 2021902885

10 9 8 7 6 5 4 3 2

45 Alternate Press, LLC
www.45alternate.com

PRAISE FOR KEEP IT 100

These stories may be brief, but they are so substantial they get deep down into your bones and bubble up into your thoughts as you move through the day. I'm amazed that Ran Walker can stuff so much meaning and power into so few words, but he does it one hundred times in *Keep in 100*. He's just that talented. To paraphrase Ethridge Knight: Making jazz swing in one hundred words AIN'T no square writer's job.

— RION AMILCAR SCOTT, AWARD-WINNING AUTHOR OF *INSURRECTIONS* AND *THE WORLD DOESN'T REQUIRE YOU*

"Keep It 100" means to keep it real. What's realer than a growing artist advancing a new style? With this collection, Ran Walker gels thematically and structurally with stories that bridge from the page, across one's imagination, and into that place all writers want to go—the heart. Now that's real."

— SABIN PRENTIS, AUTHOR OF *BETTER LEFT UNSAID* AND *COMPARED TO WHAT?*

Ran Walker excels at cross-threading various genres into bite-sized, literary wonders. Walker's passions are on full display: hip hop, superheroes, romance, families, dystopian futures, and more. A forward-thinking yet entertaining collection of microfiction.

— SCOTT SEMEGRAN, AWARD-WINNING AUTHOR OF *THE BENEVOLENT LORDS OF SOMETIMES ISLAND* AND *TO SQUEEZE A PRAIRIE DOG*

Tender and strange, startling and lyrical, witty and nuanced, Ran Walker's stories lingered in my mind long after I finished reading them. His prose is taut, precise, and economical, but each one of these tiny stories is expansive in the way it enlarges the world through an eclectic mixture of distinctive characters and surprising plots. I'm never quite at ease in a Ran Walker story. And that's a good thing. He's a master of the 100-word form.

— GRANT FAULKNER, EXECUTIVE DIRECTOR OF NANOWRIMO AND CO-FOUNDER OF *100 WORD STORY*

Ran Walker is a writer's writer. In *Keep It 100*, he brings forth so many styles, the reader is virtually assured to experience delight. This book offers a mosaic of lives lived. I will read it again and again and again.

— MAURICE CARLOS RUFFIN, AUTHOR OF *THE ONES WHO DON'T SAY THEY LOVE YOU* AND *WE CAST A SHADOW*

In almost as few words as it will take me to write this, Ran Walker gave us all the elements of good fiction: character, setting, mood, theme and strong, unique points-of-view. I admit, I was skeptical about microfiction of about one hundred words being an effective vehicle to deliver a complete story, but damned if he didn't pull it off. Exceptional.

— NIA FORRESTER, BESTSELLING AUTHOR OF
THE *COMMITMENT* SERIES

Ran Walker, like a master butcher, cuts the fat and gets to the "meat" of things. A buffet of brilliance, *Keep It 100* is a true example of great writing that can be/should be consumed and appreciated many times over.

— VAN G. GARRETT, AWARD-WINNING
AUTHOR OF *WATER BODIES* AND *SONGS IN BLUE NEGRITUDE*

We live in an age where literature is changing. Ran Walker is a champion of and innovator in the form of microfiction. *Keep It 100* is a bright and inspiring continuation of this journey. Modern voices require modern formats, and Ran has brought both together in this book.

— MITCHELL DAVIS, CEO OF BIBLIOLABS

KEEP IT 100

100-WORD STORIES

RAN WALKER

CONTENTS

PREFACE

Why write a story with only 100 words?

I came across this form when I first started exploring microfiction. Soon after, I discovered Grant Faulkner's book *Fissures* and his journal *100 Word Story*. I didn't immediately write a 100-word story, though. There was a part of me that still couldn't see how to use that amount of space to tell a story.

Still wanting to learn to write microfiction, I opted to spend more time writing 50-Word stories (often called "dribbles"), which were slightly longer than a poetic form I had been practicing called the Kwansaba (poems with 7 lines, 7 words per line, and no more than 7 letters per word). I ended up writing a book of 50-word stories titled *The Strange Museum*, and then I slowly returned my attention to writing 100-word stories.

I am grateful for writers like Robert Scotellaro, Paul Strohm, Grant Faulkner, Lydia Davis, Desiree Cooper, Diane Williams, John Edgar Wideman, Ernest Hemingway, Ana María Shua, Nancy Stohlman, and Meg Pokrass for laying out a blueprint for how one can approach microfiction. I continue to discover new microfictionists and prose poets everyday, and I am heartened that this is a form of writing that will continue on, gaining more and more recognition.

I have learned a great deal from undertaking the challenge of not only writing stories in this form, but accumulating enough work to constitute a collection. It is my sincerest hope that you will enjoy this book and that it will take your mind to unexpected and entertaining places.

Ran Walker

AUTHOR'S NOTE

Some of the works included in this collection are inspired by the works of other writers. I have, however, taken measures to ensure that my stories are not direct derivative works of stories that are still protected by U.S. copyright laws.

For Chad, Kobe, and DOOM

"A novel is just a story that hasn't yet discovered a way to be brief."

— George Saunders

PART 1

1

DUMAS

Mrs. Miller had asked her eleventh grade students to give a report on an assigned writer. She tossed surnames at them with the air of a person who'd been teaching the same subject *the same way* for twenty-five years.

Kendrick had gotten Dumas.

As Mrs. Miller sat back, preparing to hear about *The Three Musketeers* for the umpteenth time, she found herself learning about a Black writer named Henry Dumas, who'd been killed by transit cops in 1968, a writer Toni Morrison once called an "absolute genius," a writer, whom, up until that moment, Mrs. Miller had never known existed.

THE OTHER SIDE OF MADISON

(AFTER WILLIAM FAULKNER)

GRANDPA TOBIAS WOULD TELL us about his time working at the Henderson House on the other side of Madison. He'd worked there since before the old man died and swore the daughter didn't have any skills besides being a Souther belle—which wasn't worth much.

Grandpa Tobias had to damn near brush her teeth for her, to hear him tell it.

"But it wasn't all her fault," he offered. "She ain't have nobody to love on her. That'll make folks do crazy things."

We swore we could see just a hint of horror behind his eyes when he said that.

SCREAMIN' SISYPHUS

(AFTER JAY HAWKINS)

THE GODS WERE WICKED INDEED. Jalacy had intended his song to be a beautiful ballad—had even recorded a version that way—but then he got drunk during the recording session. Blacked out. Couldn't remember a thing of the hit song he'd written. Even had to relearn that drunken version the white kids liked so much.

He would later add props to spice up the performance, but there'd be no real hits after that. No redemption for a classically-trained singer.

No. He'd have to grunt at a cigarette-smoking skull for the rest of his days, laboring beneath a forgotten moment.

4

THE WATCHERS

HE COULD FEEL THEM WATCHING, their eyes moving across his brown body as he went about his daily activities, peeking at him from supermarket shelves, drugstore counters, bodegas, and neighborhood murals. They were definitely there—*of that he was convinced*—though he didn't know *why* they were there or *what* they wanted from him.

Maybe it was curiosity. That was the optimistic side of him considering the possibilities. He elected not to allow himself to consider anything more sinister, more probable.

Instead, he would ignore them and continue to move through the world, attempting to maintain a façade of freedom.

ALL WHITE MALE AUTHORS LOOK ALIKE

SHE BOUGHT him a book by John Barth as a birthday gift.

"You like him, don't you?" she asked.

He didn't know how to tell her that it was Donald Barthelme whom he enjoyed. Barth. Barthelme. Yeah, they sounded similar. But then there were Frederick, Steven, and Donald Barthelme, each with his own unique style, not unlike Barth, but it was Donald's minimalist absurdism that he loved most.

He looked at the cover (Tidewater having since evolved into Hampton Roads, with hopes of becoming "The 757") and nodded. After all, he had nothing against Barth.

"It's perfect," he responded, smiling.

THE GREAT EMANCIPATOR

(FOR ROALD DAHL)

WHEN RICKY TOWNES married Ebony Jackson and moved her into the great chocolate factory, the African pygmies rejoiced. Ricky hadn't been a bad master, but they sensed Ebony, being a Black American, might sympathize with their plight.

And she did.

It took quite a few conversations—some of them heated—but Ebony ultimately convinced Ricky that what the old candymaker had been doing amounted to slavery, that the workers had been taken from their native land to work in a factory where they'd been paid with chocolate.

Soon they were liberated and turned loose to explore the rest of England.

MOJO VS. LEGBA, PT. 1

MOJO JONES KNEW what he wanted before he even sat down at the card table to play. He knew he'd have to lose a few hands, then win a few hands, eventually getting past the scratch on the table. It was the guitar he wanted, that magnificent, brown beauty resting against the wall. Its owner had to be desperate enough to wager it.

Mojo hadn't recognized Legba, but Legba had recognized him and was more than willing to part with the instrument.

That night the bluesman would leave with the guitar, but Legba would leave with something far, far greater.

MOJO VS. LEGBA, PT. 2

YEARS AFTER MOJO had had his tiny taste of success, had drunk away his royalties, lost his old lady to the sugar, and generally made a mess of what remained, he thought back to the pocket rockets that had forced his opponent to fold. The aces were lucky, he'd figured, but now it seemed as though his luck had run its course. Without warning, he knew he would see that man again, the man who'd always stood just outside of his dreams, the man who was waiting patiently to take him past the crossroads into the wasteland of bluesman's bones.

9

THE AFTERMATH

(AFTER SHIRLEY JACKSON)

ONCE THE LAST of the stones tore loose the remaining flesh above her frozen and defocused eyes, the men of the village quickly collected her body and carried it over to a hastily constructed pyre. This part of the ritual was largely regarded as an afterthought, although it was still necessary to complete the sacrifice.

Wiping sweat from his brow, Mr. Bennington lit the single match he'd been carrying, and with one arm draped across his boys' shoulders, he said goodbye to his wife and tossed the flame onto the kindling.

But by this time, the villagers had already dispersed.

BLACK SKIN, WHITE PEN

THE WHITE SOUTHERN writers wrote about Black people as if they were a Greek chorus, quietly navigating the outer edges of their stories, either co-signing on the decisions of white characters or expressing skepticism (but never publicly). Oftentimes only a handful of Black people were given names, usually the ones who were most useful to white characters. The writers viewed this as necessary for the sake of verisimilitude, but the fact was that they simply were not interested in these characters, beyond the "color" they added to their stories. The characters, however, prayed one day someone would write *their* stories.

THREE BOOKS

SURE, many of the English majors at Wilson-Reed College had read works by George Orwell, Octavia Butler, and Margaret Atwood before, but they had never read them assembled together in one course, until they took Dr. Regina Cabello's Survey of Protest Literature.

When word of the curriculum made its way around campus, the board of trustees wrestled to find a loophole that would strip Dr. Cabello of both her tenure and job. Eventually they were successful.

By that time, though, her many students had learned, firsthand, the lessons of it all and were already preparing themselves to join the fight.

12

PARABLE OF THE PROTESTER

TERESA DREW the large letters across the back of the library using chalk. Up until that moment, she'd never protested any of the myriad of injustices, despite her growing need to take action. It was the work of Octavia Butler that caused her to sit up and maintain a vigilant awareness of the struggle of her people, and her words would be the weapon she would use to strike a blow for the cause.

She knew a bucket of water and a hard scrub could easily wash away the words, but before they acted, they'd have to read them first.

LEX TALIONIS

Toni Morrison hadn't intended to write a novel that would affect people the way J.D. Salinger's *The Catcher in the Rye* did, the kind of book that would take control of young men's imaginations, causing them to search the darker parts of their souls and emerge, weapons in hand, poised to strike, to bring about balance to the world, a sense of fairness.

The protests were destined to evolve (or devolve) into a playground where the Seven Days turned into weeks, months, and years.

Their defense, in the manner of Chapman and Hinckley, would be this: read *Song of Solomon*.

THE UNDERGROUND

(AFTER FYODOR DOSTOEVSKY, RICHARD WRIGHT, AND
RALPH ELLISON)

I HAD TO ADMIT I, too, had succumbed to the idea of living underground, on the fringes of the cacophony that is society. I chose to join the invisible streams that move around, beneath, and across the boots of the capitalist Game Masters who seek to control our ebbs and flows.

Like Bruce Lee, we have become shapeless, our water shifting and changing, gaining strength. And though we are underground, one day we will recede from those boots, leaving bare a dry ground, only to thunder back moments later as the tsunami that will bring the giants to their knees.

POSTHUMOUS

IF THE TRUTH BE TOLD, it was a meandering mess of over a thousand pages, but no one could deny that he'd written it, that he'd toiled over it for decades, that he'd intended it to be his magnum opus.

In the end, it mattered only that he was dead—and that the book was eventually published.

A public so thirsty for his work would make sense of it, propel it to the top of the bestseller lists, nudge the critics on how it should be received and interpreted, and color the mess so that it shined like a trophy.

VIRTUAL INSANITY

(AFTER JAY KAY)

It MIGHT'VE BEEN A MORE complicated, belabored decision had James decided to stay—but he didn't—so it was all on Lakeisha to make the decision, which wasn't really much of a decision, as far as she was concerned.

The procedure would alter several of the baby's genes: guarantee a "Y" chromosome, reduce the skin's melanin content, isolate the genes for straight hair, a thin nose—the best of the European features that composed only a small fraction of her (and James's) DNA.

She would have to teach him how to be white, though. That would be the hardest part.

THAT'S BETWEEN Y'ALL AND GOD

(AFTER ZORA NEALE HURSTON)

DORIS BURIED Cedric because it was what wives did for their husbands, even if they were the kinds of men who stepped out on their wives. She'd paid for the funeral with money she'd earned from laundering white folk's clothes, something Cedric had despised. She figured she would make sure he had a decent burial, but the rest was between him and God.

She felt nothing as the casket was lowered into the earth, but Big Wanda, Cedric's mistress, wailed beneath her black veil. Doris thought about pushing her into the hole, but that was between Big Wanda and God.

TEARS IN THE FABRIC OF US

(AFTER KATE CHOPIN)

HER PLAN HAD ALWAYS BEEN to outlive him. She was from a generation where you hunkered down and picked up the broken dishes, kept a smile on your face for the kids, then busied yourself with clubs that were filled with women who were doing the same.

They'd never been compatible, always trying to avoid a third rail that triggered one interminable argument. Even as she approached her 52nd anniversary, she prayed for freedom.

Early that morning, she woke to find he'd died in his sleep. Everyone assumed her flood of tears was from grief.

She was fine with that.

THE GIRL IN VERNON PARK

SHE VAGUELY REMEMBERED MEETING the woman when she was eight. She was sitting on a swing in Vernon Park, staring up into the dusky sky, when the woman had approached. She couldn't remember what the woman had said, though.

Now, thirty years later she found herself walking back toward Vernon Park, where the younger version of herself sat on a swing, staring up into the dusky sky. She had to warn the little girl about the impending danger, how humans would have to leave Earth or jump through time to avoid its fate.

She hoped she wouldn't forget this time.

DUMILE

(AFTER MF DOOM)

DANIEL FELT MISUNDERSTOOD, like Dr. Doom.

Was the Marvel character really an irredeemable, unrelenting supervillain out to destroy? After all, Dr. Doom had his own country, the Kingdom of Latveria, and ridiculous technology that rivaled (perhaps surpassed) Tony Stark's.

Daniel realized who people thought the hero was depended primarily on who told the story. A metal face could protect your identity, mask your persona, and hide your true feelings, and when people can't read your face, they fear you, as if you were a hefty, middle-aged Black man armed only with a microphone and an Akai MPC 2000XL sequencer.

PART 2

COLORFUL

SEEKING to add to his budding authorial legend, Princeton Watts planned to acquire a pet of sufficient exoticism. Flannery O'Connor kept a yard full of peacocks, and Salvatore Dalí enjoyed strutting an anteater down the sidewalk, so whatever Princeton acquired had to be shocking.

Having grown up on *The Dark Crystal*, he selected the cassowary, an enormous colorful bird that resembled a Skeksis. The bird was perfect for a fantasy writer.

He understood his mistake only when he watched the bird withdraw its long claw from his abdomen after an attempted feeding, his blood just another color among the feathers.

MUSE

THE OLD POET never tired of writing about her. His pen strokes would capture the way her eyes glanced at him and her lips turned upward into an asymmetrical smile; the way she would touch her ear delicately as she giggled at one of his random musings; the way her thick, brown curls gently brushed the hairs of his arms; the way her dark, strong legs felt wrapped around his hips; the way her tongue danced upon his flesh like a wet feather; the way her breath tickled his ear; and the melodious way in which she said his name.

THE LIBRARIES

I ONCE WALKED into a small Southern town that had more libraries than churches. There were three or four of them on each street. Occasionally I'd mistake one for a small house, then see the letters for Brautigan or Borges or Baldwin or Brontë adorning the entrance. Their parking lots were full of bicycles and mopeds, and out back, beneath a tarp, people lay on their backs, barefoot, books covering their faces like masks.

I approached the main branch downtown, where a librarian greeted me at the door.

"Welcome," she said.

It was then that I knew I'd never leave.

FASHION AND THE ART OF READING

To ASSURE that she read the book, she refused to put it on her shelf after she purchased it. Instead, she carried it from room to room, setting it on the sofa arm or the dining room table. She even placed it in her purse to carry with her, just in case a moment presented itself for her to read it, maybe standing in line at a store or while rolling through an automated carwash. She occasionally finished a page or two, never really putting a dent in the book, which she gradually accepted had become merely a fashion accessory.

STRUCTURE

SOME DAYS NORMAN wished he lived within the sterile, clean lines of a Chris Ware drawing, where everything was in its own proper compartment, the overlap of fall colors washing over everything. There would be a Wes Anderson type of milieu where things were ironic in an *ironic* type of way, the conflicts far more controlled and internal.

But, no, Norman's world was wide open, no lines framing things, holding them in place, anchoring people to a principle, just miles of randomness and chaos, a world content on doing *whatever* it wanted, *whenever* it wanted, its structure long ago abandoned.

TSUNDOKU

THOUSANDS of them stared at her from their respective slots on their shelves, all unopened, save the occasional bookmark a sales associate might have slid into them at the register, clinging to the scent of the printing facility from which they were shipped, spines taut and uncracked, frozen in their places and adored from a distance.

They watched her walk into the apartment staring at her phone, then change into a long t-shirt and watch the 55" TV in her den.

Mute, they were the wall behind her, welcoming new members, none of them apparently interesting enough to be read.

LA TRADUCTORA

SHE WAS KNOWN throughout the industry for translating renowned books from the Spanish language, but few knew of her failed attempts at getting her slim English-language novel published in America.

Publishers regarded the length as too short and the plot as too whimsical. And there was no point in getting started on the magical realism that seemed to leap from every other page.

So the translator decided to slap a pseudonym on her miniature manuscript and developed a story that it was an unearthed, previously unpublished work by a Borges protégé, whereupon she easily sold it in under a month.

THAT COLOSSAL WRECK

(AFTER L. FRANK BAUM)

Oz WAS nothing like her mother had described it. Graffiti overran the city. Winged monkeys sat by idly smoking cigarettes. Munchins lazed about, some of them shooting dice on the corner, others just standing around like people lost in a bad dream. The wizard had long ago left *(had even returned to politics!)*, and with him, all the hopes of the city.

But Liza was a fighter, just like her mother, and had decided that she would stay and make things right. The citizens of Oz needed someone to believe in, so she set off for the wizard's throne room.

THE BANNED BOOK CLUB

THE BANNED BOOK Club began as a fierce reaction to the Oak Bluff school board's decision to ban a list of 100 literary classics from the shelves of all of the school libraries, including the high school, where students were vocal about some of their favorite YA books being eighty-sixed.

Even more interesting, the book club chose to meet at the public library branch in town, where they moved, one by one, through the list of banned books.

Eventually, the school librarians posted flyers for the club's meeting times on their doors.

The school board simply pretended not to notice.

BACKWARD PEOPLE

IT WAS no secret that the smaller a town was, the deeper its secrets ran. Those attempts at presenting a pure morality, an idyllic Norman Rockwell painting, were deliberate in order to mask the darkness that lurked beneath their façades of smiling cherubs sipping milkshakes on spinning drugstore stools, a sinister apothecary smiling in the background, his hand resting inconspicuously on the waist of the adolescent girl serving them. Whether it was William Faulkner or Grace Metalious, the stories would be told, and a public oblivious to its own demons would savor those tales, enthusiastically entertained by those backward people.

THE NOVEL

EVEN AS HE stood before the Alexandre Literary Award Committee, and all of the literati who had traveled far and wide to see him accept his award, he still couldn't, for the life of him, figure out how he had won such a prestigious award without remembering ever having written the book.

He had quizzed his ex-girlfriend, the agent who'd released him from his contract, and the editor who'd rejected his last book. Surely they'd know.

They were unanimous that he'd written the book and also that his understanding of them was completely erroneous.

Reluctantly, he chose to believe.

METROPHOBIA

He'd planned to impress her by taking her to the open mic over at Dino's and performing a poem he'd written for her.

The emcee allowed him to go first. However, when he stood before her, he sensed dread in her eyes. *She thinks I'm going to embarrass her,* he thought, *but she doesn't realize how good I am.*

He started the poem.

Caught up in his words, he mistook her tears for joy. Afterwards, she politely excused herself. She considered telling him the truth, about her fear of poetry, but he'd already made an assumption he couldn't walk back.

INEFFABILITY

HE WAS a poet who wrote whenever the muse struck him, writing purely off inspiration. She was a novelist who sat at her desk, regardless of her mood, and wrote her two thousand words each day.

Each of his critically-acclaimed collections were less than a hundred pages. Each of her bestselling novels exceeded three hundred pages.

He wrote his poems longhand, using a pencil and an old composition notebook. She typed all of her stories using a MacBook Pro.

Creatively, they could hardly be more different, yet the life they shared was beautiful beyond either's ability to frame in words.

DESTINY OF THE DAMNED

THE FACE-OFF WAS in the making for nearly two decades. No one knew this, of course *(how could they?)*, but all the same, these two people were destined to cross paths on the campus of State University, where things would come to a head.

The two individuals: Susan Parker, the quintessential teacher's sycophant who sat not only on the front row, but in the middle of the room; and Dr. Marcellus Winston Mathews, an astute, although somewhat punctilious professor who was by far the most sialoquent member of the faculty.

The only real question: would she stay when he sprayed?

THE RECONCEPTUALIZATION OF
REBECCA HAWTHORNE

SHE'D BEEN LAUDED as one of the greatest writers of the 21st century, had received many of the major literary awards, had received three honorary doctorates, and had even received the Presidential Medal of Freedom.

It was only when a womanist scholar from Howard University brought to the public's attention the author had never used a non-white character in any of her work, not even in passing, that things shifted entirely.

Was she really a writer of her times, an artist poised to lead the canon forward, or was she the embodiment of a nostalgia reserved solely for the privileged?

88 KEYS

Ms. Brigette would sometimes pop Marilyn's wrists lightly with a wooden ruler.

"You must arch your hands, not flatten them," she'd say, before adjusting her bifocals.

Marilyn would straighten her back and adjust her hands over the keys and continue her scales.

The deal Marilyn had made with her mother was that she'd take lessons for a year. Then, if she still wanted to learn to play by ear (like her favorite songwriters), her mother would acquiesce.

Sometimes Marilyn wondered what had led the old woman to teach piano lessons.

Maybe there was a time Ms. Brigette, too, wanted more.

BUCKROE

TERRY CONTINUED to unwind his kite as it sailed higher and higher against the burnt orange of the sunset. Coltrane, his Lab, had given up chasing after it, choosing instead to trot along the coastline, its paws tracking the sand like musical notes.

That evening Terry would get his weekly phone call from his mother and how she worried about him being single at his age. But she couldn't see the sunset, the kite drifting toward the violet of dusk, or Coltrane nestling against his calves as he stood there with the sand between his toes.

He was just fine.

SCHADENFREUDE

THE PROFESSOR PREFERRED to use the word "epicari-cacy," which he found to move a bit easier in his mouth. That was what his adversaries thrived upon, he told his students. "They want so desperately to dance upon my grave," he mentioned one day, apropos of nothing.

What he failed to realize was that many of the students privately wished he would tumble down the stairs of the lecture hall and break his neck. Others simply thought of him as a pedantic jackass. But all of them had selected the shoes they would wear as they danced alongside his smiling colleagues.

UNPLUGGED

SOMETIMES I WONDER if it's possible to be a writer and not be on social media. You'll hear, from time to time, stories about how Jonathan Franzen despises it or how Zadie Smith doesn't even own a smartphone. It's the classic writer's fantasy where you find a little shack where you either write longhand with a pencil and a notebook or type away on an old typewriter, the pages accumulating at your feet. Nowhere in this fantasy is there room for the misspent energy of social media, each letter of each word carefully crafted onto the page for art's sake.

THE MOUSE

WE MARVELED at how the mouse's palate must have been far more sophisticated than the peanut butter and cheddar cheese we'd been placing on the traps. We began to experiment with different cheeses, exotic and imported, eager to find something it might like. Just as we were lost in our experiments—and had long since deemed the idea of trapping and killing the mouse futile (and even barbaric)—we focused our energies on trying to find a way to please it.

It never ate the cheese, though, which led us to slowly wonder if the mouse was ever really there.

PART 3

THE SCIENCE OF RELATIONSHIPS

HER HEARTBEAT PULSED ECSTATICALLY beneath his ear, as he tasted the softness of her skin. Even naked, she didn't consider this act as being unfaithful to her boyfriend hundreds of miles away. There would, of course, be no intercourse, just heavy petting, and maybe occasional dinners, ice skating in Central Park, and nights lying in bed discussing her dreams.

No. She was passing the time while in grad school. For all she knew, her boyfriend might be doing the same.

Her true future was an alternate reality in a different state, a solid, where this experience was merely a liquid.

AUTUMN (REDUX)

THE SUN GLOWED in the dew of the morning grass, and a gentle breeze tickled her arm and danced in the curls of her hair.

Even the leaves were starting to change colors, slowly shifting from greens, blues, and yellows into oranges, browns, and reds. Maybe she'd buy a few pumpkins to sit on the porch as decorations or put up a seasonal wreath and a garland of leaves.

This was her favorite time of year, the season for which she was named, and although she now stayed indoors because of the pandemic, her love of autumn would never change.

BROOKLYN IN FALL

HER VOICE CARRIED on the October breeze, a melody against the city's chords, car horns and swearing cabdrivers kicking the bass drum, industrious construction workers slapping the snare. She whispered aspirations, desires, confessions, each exhalation a note that drifted upward through the milieu of the maze, finding its way into the open window of an apartment on the third floor of a Park Slope brownstone.

There Evan tip-toed up his bedroom wall, dancing on the ceiling, his syncopated steps sensing a groove only his heart could understand.

His mother had warned him falling in love would feel this way.

44

TWO DAYS LATER

HE HADN'T ENVISIONED it as a one-night stand, but she hadn't returned any of his calls or texts, yet.

During the moment, it had seemed like she was really into him: they'd both taken turns climaxing as the night lights of the city drifted through his blinds like constellations.

Constellations? Maybe that was a bit too cliché.

Still, there was a magic there, a chemistry that seemed like a foundation worth building upon.

Now that the experience had become nudiustertian, he wondered if maybe that was all there would ever be. He hoped not, but it wasn't up to him.

45

THE REVELATION

WE DISCOVERED, in the weeks that followed the great novelist's death, that he'd accumulated a massive collection of handwritten leatherbound journals, each page filled with his tiny cursive and copious, pensive ideas, top to bottom, despite his having published only two novels during his lifetime.

We'd assumed he'd given up on writing after that last book, but these volumes told a different story.

As we went through the tedious, but intriguing, process of reading his words, we came to understand his reason for never writing another book: he couldn't live up to our expectations, so he refused to even try.

OBJECTIVELY SPEAKING

OBJECTIVELY SPEAKING, I can say he was not the finest of writers, but he did have an enormous vocabulary and a plethora of opinions, two things, like smoke and mirrors, that, when used together, often presented the illusion of literary genius. He was above plot, above logic; his role was to speak his unadulterated truth from his purple-prosed throne, ensconced in his ivory tower.

Hell, he could have done this all day, baffling the literary boys' club with his bullshit. In that, he truly was an artist of the highest order. So that, my dear reader, is what he did.

MUTUAL MEDITATIONS

THEY HAD AGREED upon mutual meditations: she found her solace in handwashing the modest number of dishes that accumulated every few days; he found his solace in attacking the lawn with the old push mower, the grass never growing beyond the length of his fingers.

Since the pandemic had dictated the governor issue a "stay-at-home" order, they spent far more time together than they reasoned any happily married couple should.

At first things were refreshing, reminiscent of their honeymoon; then they began to trip over each other.

But there were always dishes that needed washing and grass that needed cutting.

GRANDMA'S PHOTOGRAPH

GRANDMA ESTELLE HAS a picture of a strange man hanging above the mantle in her living room. She'd found the picture shortly after Grandpa John passed. She claims that the strange man had appeared to her in her dreams and told her to hang his picture. Fighting her fears, she did as she was told, or so she says.

Of course, there're a few of us who believe the photograph is of a man she once pined for before her marriage to Grandpa John, but we keep this to ourselves.

The picture makes her happy, so we let it be.

KAWAII

THE KIDS at the boarding school had managed to find hundreds of ways of calling Akari ugly to the point she would use the spending money her parents sent her to buy dolls and other items that would help cocoon her in cuteness while she sat alone in her dorm room.

She kept to herself so they wouldn't make fun of her eyes or make jokes about how she spoke (even though her diction was identical to theirs).

One night she awakened to a chorus of dolls praising her beauty through tiny mouths.

Things would be different now, she knew.

A FIRST KISS, CIRCA 1990

HE SAT on top of a picnic table, and she stood between his legs, her back resting on his chest. The stars sparkled in the summer sky, a chorus of encouragement, a nearby light pole giving them a spotlight.

They'd been talking on the phone every night for two weeks, so she'd finally agreed to meet him in the park.

She was older by two years, but he had still managed to get her attention, although he didn't know how he'd managed that.

His heart now beating through his face, he leaned in to kiss her.

She responded in kind.

THE YARBOROUGH

HIS GIRLFRIEND TOLD him the best way to get in good with her father was to play Spades with him. No problem.

He quickly discovered the old man didn't play with jokers and kept all of the deuces at the bottoms of their suits. Fine, he could play that way.

Halfway through the game, though, he was dealt a hand that didn't have any face cards or spades, so he tossed his hand onto the middle of the table face-up.

Later when his girlfriend recounted the evening, she explained his faux pas. "We always play through. We never give up."

BENEATH THE WAVES

RICO THOUGHT the stories were just urban legends the older lifeguards told the newbies just to mess with them, some friendly hazing for the uninitiated. Sometimes the stories were delivered with a straight face, other times with a sinister smirk or a cartoon villain's "heh heh heh."

Then one evening while on patrol, Rico noticed something—*someone*—emerging from the waves in the distance. She hadn't been there a moment ago.

He grabbed a flotation ring and ran toward the shoreline. Stepping into the water, he saw her head go under, then her tail rise above the surface before submerging.

DEATH AND THE TSUNAMI

THE CLOAKED figure stood by patiently waiting. Twenty years ago people would have stared in fascination, watching the receding water pull away from the shoreline. He would come through and claim several of them once the water made landfall.

Now, with the advent of smartphones, the kids stared at the water much longer, each trying to catch the perfect video of the phenomenon, in hopes of getting more "likes," he reckoned.

They made his job far too easy these days, actually took away much of the fun. Sure, he would take them with the water, but it wasn't the same.

APOCALYPTIC AMBIVALENCE

EACH DAY the horrors they woke to grew exponentially: the community water jugs had been stolen by marauders, food had grown scarcer, and some of them were now too sick to move.

McKafree had considered running away and taking his chances in the Desert of Death, beyond the Fellowship Walls, but the thought of facing the horrors out there by himself was scarier than the horrors themselves.

He'd stay put, nursing the sick, praying for the gods to release the rains and to strike down their enemies. He'd do what he'd always done, what he'd been trained to do: nothing.

PICKENS COUNTY

THE WHITE TOWNSPEOPLE chased Henry up to the second floor of the building, cornering him in a small room. The thunder outside the window rumbled like a stampeding herd of elephants. Lightning flashed its wicked grin as it kissed the glass panes. The mob still believed he'd burned down the previous courthouse and were determined to take their justice.

And they did—but not before the lightning could record Henry's face in the window.

Now the descendants of those townspeople walk around telling ghost stories about Henry Wells, pointing out his likeness at dusk to any tourist wandering through Carrollton.

ERIC'S THINGS, CIRCA 1985

ERIC'S FAMILY rolled into Tupelo like a tornado, and by sunset, Reggie was homeless.

The lawyer told Reggie since everything the couple had acquired was in Eric's name, legally Eric owned it, and without a will, the law dictated Eric's family would get the assets Reggie had contributed to over the years.

Reggie pleaded with them to keep a few things, like the Oldsmobile only he'd driven, but they denied him, as they had their son when he was alive.

They burned Eric's things and sold the house, but they could never find the car—although they had their suspicions.

ONE HOUR

THE TIME MACHINE HAD WORKED, but it would only allow him a one-hour roundtrip. With that hour he had considered many things: visiting the Twin Towers once more, warning people of the things that would happen over the next decade, eating a meal at his favorite defunct restaurant, or buying stocks in companies that had yet to get big.

But only one thought dominated his thoughts: finding his mother so he could hold her, listen to her, laugh with her. The cancer would come back in two years and take her away, but he had bought himself one more hour.

AN EXPERIMENT

IN AN EXPERIMENT HOUSED in the department of psychology at State University, a random group of students, all of different ethnic backgrounds, were hypnotized and told they belonged to a different ethnic group. Many of the students behaved the same as they always had, while others immediately took on affectations of stereotypes they'd associated with those groups.

Later as they watched a video of their actions, Bramble Lindbergh thought it was hilarious that he'd used the n-word so many times, all while grabbing at his genitals. The others, however, stared on in horror, afraid of what this experiment might represent.

THE TRAILER

(FOR NICHELLE NICHOLS)

MOST OF THEM weren't even there to see the movie; they were there to see the world debut of the trailer for the *Galaxy Fighters* final installment. This was something Jalen was looking forward to sharing with his daughter, especially after talking up the series.

Then it happened. A Black woman appeared on the screen, bold and beautiful, ready to kick ass, the first to ever appear in the series.

Later the trolls would complain on social media about "diversity," but in that moment Jalen tried to hold back tears as he gazed at the wonder in his daughter's eyes.

NUMBERS

JOSH ALWAYS WATCHED the lottery alone, his door locked to keep out his roommates. He'd been playing the same number for ten years, and after writing down Saturday's numbers, he checked his ticket against them ten times. He had thought if the moment ever came he'd scream, maybe dance. Now he sat holding his winning ticket, terrified.

$825,000,000.

What on earth would he do with that? And what about when his family and friends came for him? Could he trust anyone anymore?

He quickly endorsed the back of the ticket and quietly checked the internet for tickets to Australia.

PART 4

FEAR

AFTER DECADES of writing horror and selling millions of books, Winston Knight had grown synonymous with the genre. People wore his likeness on their t-shirts, carried around action figures of him—some even wore tattoos.

He'd written books about murderers, monsters, aliens, and clowns, none of which scared him in the least. He carried only one fear with him, the one that persistently fueled his career. Even at age 70, he could see, very clearly, his intoxicated father standing in the darkened doorway of his childhood room, holding a freshly unplugged iron, its handle resting anxiously in those meaty palms.

62

TENTACLES

SHORTLY AFTER HIS PARENTS DIVORCED, Anon began to have Lovecraftian nightmares, where he would be lying in his bed and tentacles would slide out from beneath the frame and wrap themselves tightly across his chest. He would awaken panting, the pressure still pulsing deep within his muscles.

He took to reading from an old joke book before going to bed, but when he turned off the lights and closed his eyes, his mind turned toward the deity he believed lived beneath his mattress.

It was a strange place for a monster to be: beneath the bed of a grown man.

PRESTIDIGITATION

HE'D LEARNED several tricks with pieces of silver and other smaller objects during his travels to other lands. By the time he made it home, he was a master of prestidigitation and quickly set out to entertain his people.

Their reactions astonished him. They each asked him to repeatedly perform various tricks—*miracles* they called them. Many craved to be near him, while others despised his abilities.

Fearing for his safety, he escaped during the middle of the night to find another place to dwell. But his countrymen would continue to talk about his miracles many generations after he'd left.

THE LAST STAND

FATIGUE ENCASING HIS LEGS, Diego shuffled along, knowing the monster was near. Darkness covered the trees, and he could now hear his heavy breathing mixed with the chirps of crickets.

Then the thunderous thumps of something tearing a path through the broken limbs snapped him to attention.

He had no strength to climb and no energy to continue running. With few options left, he grabbed his knife, found a hollowed log, and climbed inside.

As the beast drew near, sensing the man had stopped running, it looked around, its teeth bared.

They knew only one would emerge from the forest.

THE CONFESSIONS OF PAPA BEAR

WHO THE HELL does this little girl think she is? Oh, the privilege! Seriously, how is this little white girl going to break into our house; sit all over our furniture; eat our food (or pick at it), leaving her little germs on our spoons; and then sleep in our beds? She acts like she owns the place, like we are visitors in our own damn house.

I would call the cops, but you know how they can be, especially because we're brown and apparently look dangerous.

Next time she breaks in, we will just have to handle this ourselves.

THE OTHER SIDE OF THE WALL

RORY SAT PATIENTLY, spinning the ·thick wooden handle in his hands. Occasionally he glanced at the monitor, then the large digital clock on the wall. *He* would never pay to come to a place like this, but he didn't mind working there.

He glanced at the clock again. Five minutes left.

The teens in the escape room wrestled frantically to get out.

Rory stood, stretched his muscled frame, and hoisted the axe onto his shoulder. When the clock struck zero, he entered the room through the secret door, his axe already poised to tear through the first of the losers.

CONTRARY TO POPULAR OPINION, TED IS NOT HERE TO SAVE THE DAY

SCIENTISTS SHELVED the vaccine after it killed half of the the trial subjects and caused superhuman powers in three of the survivors. Of those survivors, one became a superhero (Ultramatic), one became a supervillain (Demonicon), and the third one (Ted, whom you've probably never heard of) elected to live a life of quiet anonymity.

Years later, after Ultramatic and Demonicon had wreaked havoc around the world in their epic battles, a journalist tracked down Ted and asked why he had never used his superpowers to get involved.

"Superpowers only make you more of what you already are," he responded apathetically.

THE TUNNEL OF YOUTH

A GUY who looked like he was sixteen helped Philip onto the only seat on the rollercoaster.

"Excuse me," Philip said, through mangled coughs. "Young man?"

"Yes, sir?" the guy responded.

"Does this ride really work? Am I really going to —cough—get back my youth and my health?"

"Definitely. I'm 95 and was terminal last year. Lung cancer, just like you."

Philip nodded.

The guy continued, "It's not so bad here. Beats the alternative."

As the car began to move, Philip considered whether death would be better than being trapped in this park forever, alongside the other lost souls.

UNDEAD

AT FIRST, most people spent too much time trying to figure out the "why" of it. Scientists proposed many hypotheses, each one more outlandish than the last, and the media made sure to run them all, keeping viewers glued to their screens. The reanimation of dead people who infected the living, however, was not a hard concept for the outliers to accept. Angel and his fellow fanboys had already raided the home supply stores, buying up every machete in sight. They were not going down without a fight, and they were prepared to decapitate anything that got in their way.

INDISPUTABLE

THE LITTLE GIRL's blood still stained the streets, one of the officer's bullet casings resting nearby, next to the grid of a gutter. Less than a block away from the caution tape, Black fists pumped the air, amid chants, and officers in riot gear stood ready, thirstily tapping their batons against huge polycarbonate shields.

No one disputed what had happened: a six-year-old girl was playing in front of her house when a botched police raid of an empty neighboring house resulted in her being shot eight times.

Everything else, however, remained open to broad interpretation, gross speculation, and political rhetoric.

IDLE HANDS

THREE WEEKS after Albert was let go from his job due to COVID-19 shutdowns, he decided to start his own religion. He'd been binging conspiracy videos on YouTube and researching the origins of certain groups. He figured he would give it a try.

Enlisting the help of a few friends, he created videos and gradually assembled "writings," which he parsed out in chatrooms. Then he launched the merchandising arm, plastering his symbols in every corner of the Internet as memes and bumper stickers, t-shirts and enamel pins.

When the pandemic eventually cleared away, he had already become a messiah.

STRANGETOWN

CORNELIUS WASN'T *SCARY* UGLY. He was what I guess you'd call normal ugly, the kind of ugly you can look at, without exactly marveling at, and know there was just enough funkiness there to tip the ugly scale.

Occasionally he would act ugly. There's that part of you, I guess, that just feels it to match the exterior, probably the reason Dinah Lefleur feels she has to go help out at the soup kitchen while wearing her sash and crown.

For most of us, ugly and pretty don't even much matter.

Hell, we're all a little strange down here.

BENEATH THE CANOPY OF THE OLD OAK TREE

I THINK about the moment we met a lot now, wondering how things might've been if you'd turned me down. Who was I to spit game in the grocery store parking lot? But you said yes.

KeKe asks me to tell her that story every night before I put her to bed.

She looks so much like you now, down to the smile.

She asked me to bring this drawing for you.

I'll leave it right here.

She asks when you'll return, and I try not to cry.

I don't know how to explain cancer to her—or to myself.

THE GIFT

HER SISTERS BOUGHT her a wig of human hair as a gift before her first round of treatments, but it felt funny on her head, so she placed it on a foam stand and named it Annalise.

At night, long after her sisters had returned to their homes, she talked to Annalise. She told Annalise the things she couldn't bring herself to tell anyone else, the fears that haunted her.

And while Annalise never said a single word in response, when she got the update from her oncologist, she wanted Annalise, above all others, to hear the good news first.

FIX ME UP

WHEN I FIRST PURCHASED THE fix-me-up, I figured I could knock out the repairs on my own within six months. It was my first home, and I was incredibly optimistic.

As it turned out, I worked on that house for many years, while living in a small apartment. Each year the house improved, while my health declined.

By the time I'd completed the restoration of the house, I'd reached a point where I could no longer enjoy it—so I sold it for a small profit.

But that pittance paled in comparison to what that house had taken from me.

ABSOLUTION

Caesar would stand in front of his bathroom mirror practicing curse words, focusing on the resonance in his thirteen-year-old voice, watching his eyes and lips to make sure he was selling it. Then, afterwards, he would pray to God to forgive him for cursing.

He hadn't quite figured out how to navigate his neighborhood and still be a good Catholic boy.

In confession each week, he would tell the priest the same thing and receive his absolution, then run home, lock himself in his bathroom and start the cycle all over again.

Survival was necessary. The streets weren't the cathedral.

THE MARRIAGE OF TWO GIFTS

NANCY CARRIED around a pocket memo notebook and a number two pencil in the small knit purse her mother had bought her for Christmas. Often, she would take it out and jot down an unusual word that she'd heard on TV or at the store, where she often eavesdropped on private conversations. When she got home, she would look up each word in the unabridged dictionary her father had bought her for Christmas and write it down neatly on each page. Occasionally, she would play with those words, shaping them into something new, something that might erase the word "divorce."

MORTAL THOUGHTS

DURING THE FIRST few weeks of the plague, he found himself having dreams of dying. He'd lost several close friends already, and he'd never felt closer to death than he did then.

Even when he was awake, he obsessed about the moment when a person passed away (or expired, depending on whom you asked). Did everything just go black? Was there a light? What was the thing that caused Steve Job's last words to be "Wow. Wow. Wow."? Did religion really matter, and if so, which one?

Then one day the plague left, and with it, all of his questions.

DARWIN

It was the summer of 2005 when Little Timothy Rothkins introduced his friends to the concept of the Darwin Awards through a paperback he'd "borrowed" from his cousin's bookshelf.

At first they wrestled to understand how it worked. How does one remove oneself from the gene pool, thereby advancing the species?

Then Timothy gave an example: "This one guy died when he accidentally shot himself in his sleep. The kicker: he was sleeping with his gun!"

None of his friends believed him. The Internet was full of those kinds of hoaxes.

Still, they were extra careful from that point forward.

A PSA FROM BONZO THE CLOWN

THE KIDS STOOD around Bonzo the Clown, waiting for him to get up. One of the kids, whose mother was a doctor, kept saying that he'd had a stroke. When they asked how she knew, she just said, "He looks stroked out."

Another kid, thinking it was a game, undid another balloon and let out the air in Bonzo's face.

It was only when one of the parents walked into the room and saw Bonzo and all the empty balloons on the floor that someone screamed.

That day they learned a new word—*asphyxiation*—and learned balloon voices weren't safe.

PART 5

IT's ALL my mother's fault. She's the one who encouraged Grandma Jo to find a hobby after Grandpa Steve passed away. Baking cookies. Golfing. Quilting. Crossword puzzles. Origami. Bingo. Scrapbooking. Really anything.

She had no idea Grandma Jo would become a sneakerhead. Now all my grandmother talks about are the latest pairs of Jordan 1 OGs she copped from some online sneaker raffle, and how all of her friends in the retirement community are now officially *dripped*.

Grandma Jo has also requested that, from here forward, our family refer to her only as Grandma Swagu, Queen of the Lace Swaps.

THE BEGINNING OF A BEAUTIFUL THING

(FOR SNEAKERHEADS)

As HE FINISHED MOWING the last yard of the summer, he let the engine run until the gas ran out. He then walked it two blocks to his house and placed it in the utility shed behind his house.

Cutting the neighbors' yards had been his father's suggestion for how he could make the money for the sneakers he wanted.

Now that he had the cash, he grabbed a quick shower and borrowed his father's hoopty and headed to the mall.

As he tried on the shoes, he had only the faintest idea of the memories he'd create in them.

SHADOWBOXING

LATE AT NIGHT Marz Banx shadowboxed in the small confines of his room, chanting cadenced rhymes with the swift movements of his hands, punctuating his breath "Morse code" style, a sheen of sweat steadily building over his body, unable to quench his need to lay some wack MC on his back, whether literally or metaphorically.

He could hear his neighbor's girlfriend moaning through the adjacent brick wall of his third floor dorm room, on the verge of exploding, but Marz kept his mind sharp, focused, his hands moving, steady, his lips in sync with each strike of his closed hands.

84

THE CYPHER (REMIXED)

THE REAL HIP hop heads on the third floor of Dubois Hall liked to rock a cypher during the witching hour, a Dilla beat turned down low to keep the RAs at bay.

Spitting from the dome, Marz would decompress from the stresses of the day, re-centering himself, not only mentally, but spatially, with the universe that spanned outside the dorm room window.

The memory of these cyphers would be the thing that anchored him years later, as he traveled from city to city (and abroad), making his dreams of becoming the dopest MC of all time a greater possibility.

A MICRO BIO OF THE LEGENDARY MARZ BANX

MARZATREK DAVID BANKS spent most of his senior year at Ellison-Wright College crafting and spitting bars over Marvin the Martian's FruityLoops beats. Until they connected during their junior year, neither had thought a music career was even possible, yet they'd met serendipitously and formed The Space Modulators, their own version of Wonder Twins (activate!), Afrofuturistic dudes back before that was really a thing. Marz had maintained a 3.6 GPA while leaving a tour's worth of open mics in his wake. If he hadn't graduated with a record deal, the plan was to teach literature. Fate, however, had other plans.

JA KENDRICK BROWN'S CARNEGIE HALL DEBUT

JA KENDRICK BROWN sat at the Steinway, his dreadlocks falling like a curtain across his face, his fingers resting gently on the keys before him. He didn't bother looking into the audience. The room was too dark, and the spotlight only illuminated where he sat. Still, he knew his family was out there.

He hummed softly to himself, something he'd begun doing to steady his nerves before performing.

He never thought he'd be in Carnegie Hall—with a full house—yet every struggle he overcame in the hard streets of New York had led him here.

He would not disappoint.

THAT ONE CHARACTER IN A JUDD APATOW MOVIE

HE WAS the kind of guy who walked around his apartment naked, farting bare-ass, then laughing heartily while stepping away to avoid the smell, the kind of guy who prided himself on how many letters of the alphabet he could unleash in a single, wet belch.

She'd left him four weeks earlier, and he'd subsequently blamed her for not loving him enough. With true love, it shouldn't matter whether you used the bathroom with the door wide open or if your lover occasionally gave you a "Dutch oven." She was too bougie for his tastes.

Real love required unadulterated acceptance.

ANOTHER CHRISTMAS STORY

IN 1986 MY parents asked me what I wanted for Christmas, so, like any other ten-year-old Black kid who watched primetime television, I asked for a Mr. T action figure. Technically it was B.A. (Bad Attitude) Baracus, the mohawked, gold-chain-wearing, muscle-bound guy from The A-Team. I didn't need the other characters. Just B.A. Baracus.

I'd make him beat up my G.I. Joe guys, leap off the porch in spectacular combat poses, and wreck shop in my little sister's Barbie Dreamhouse.

That Christmas I got school clothes instead of the action figure, and the show ended up getting cancelled.

Go figure.

BURNING CHICKEN

Naima cringed every time she saw the hashtag online: #MamaBurningChicken. She'd been trying to multitask: cook lunch, make sure her daughter wasn't having problems with her remote fifth grade classes, all while trying to participate in *her* own remote class discussion for Ellison-Wright College. There were far too many moving pieces, and somewhere along the way, she simply dropped the ball.

While responding to her history professor's question, she smelled the char coming from the kitchen, and, without thinking, blurted out, "Lord, I think I burned my chicken!"

The session was being recorded—and her classmates couldn't resist the temptation.

HAIR PROBLEMS

HER BEAUTIFUL LOCS, twisted into an elaborate braid, flowed down the wall of the tower. It had taken her an enormous amount of time to wash it, and this was the quickest and most efficient way to dry her hair.

Gazing out the window, as she waited, she could vaguely feel a tug at her scalp. She looked down and noticed there was a man climbing her hair!

"Hey! What are you doing? Get off of my hair!" she said, her eyebrows furrowed.

"But, Rapunzel, I'm here to rescue you."

"From what exactly? Boy, bye!"

Then she shook him loose.

THE COMEDIAN

AFTER YEARS of being away from the spotlight, Lip Harrison decided to return to his roots in standup comedy. He knew that he'd evolved during his downtime and was eager to test out his new material. Like Rock and Chappelle, he felt he'd graduated to a point where he could speak his version of the truth, while still making the audience laugh.

As he stood before the eager crowd, spotlight in his face, microphone in his sweaty hands, he began his routine.

No one laughed.

So in desperation, he returned to his classic fart jokes and brought down the house.

TESTICULAR FORTITUDE

BERNARD BRACED HIMSELF. He still questioned why he'd agreed to compete in this event. The gold medals weren't even made of real gold.

His success would in no way enhance his curriculum vitae. There wasn't a spot under "Awards" where The Wildman Olympics would bear any weight. This was strictly for his house and the memories they might share years from now.

Athletic cups were forbidden, as was closing your thighs prematurely.

It was a dumb game. One built on male bravado and alcohol.

He willed himself to stand still and welcome the steel-toed boot, while trying not to scream.

BIGGER

Bakari stared at the mirror, inspecting himself from every angle. He was definitely different. His johnson was bigger somehow, thicker and longer, even as he stood there completely flaccid.

"Hey, Lachelle," he called to his wife. "I want you to come here and take a look at something."

He stood in front of her, arms crossed, trying to suppress the smile on his face. "Compliments of the Negro Soulstice."

"What?" she responded before looking down. "Oh. My. God!"

"I guess *this* is my new superpower," he said chuckling coyly.

But Lachelle didn't look as happy as he'd hoped she'd be.

CRUSH(ED)

GREG HAD HARBORED a crush on Felicia for two straight summers, but his adolescent nervousness prevented him from telling a soul, let alone expressing an interest directly.

One day, however, an upperclassman named Sean called him out after school.

"You like Felicia, don't you?" Sean asked.

Greg tried to play stupid, but eventually he admitted his crush.

"You know she fucking Frank, right?"

The words hung there, burning Greg's face.

Later he would wonder if Sean had told the truth or if the upperclassman was just messing with him. Either way, Felicia now felt too far outside of his reach.

THE FLASH PROPOSAL

As THE SHE walked through the courtyard of the out-side mall, the speakers rang out with her favorite song. Moments later, people she had assumed were merely random shoppers had coalesced into a chore-ographed dance group that moved into a circle around her. Her boyfriend even joined in, his rhythm somewhat challenged and awkward, but she knew this was his idea. He was the kind of person who loved the attention, while she was not.

But still she waited patiently, as they danced for another *three minutes*, all the while trying to figure out the nicest way to say "no."

RESPECTFULLY

Dear Morgan Nelson Rachmaninoff, IV:

This letter comes on the heels of my repeated and adamant declarations that you abstain from allowing your Pembroke Welsh Corgi to defecate on my lawn.

I do understand that my house is the smallest in the subdivision, that the entirety of my house could possibly fit well within the confines of your own—with space to spare—but I see this as no reason why my lawn should be the target of your dog's hefty bowel movements.

Should I discover anymore feces, I will use it to polish your Rolls Royce.

Respectfully,
Cletus Williams

KERRI GOES TO HARVARD

THE TWINS, although identical, had been noticeably different since they were little kids, Kerri preferring dolls and princess costumes, Kierra board games and LEGOs. As they grew older, Kierra preferred absolute privacy, while Kerri longed to share the minutiae of her life on social media—which, in and of itself, was not particularly problematic, except that Kierra was often confused for Kerri.

One guy had even dismissed Kierra's body by referencing a picture Kerri had posted of herself wearing a two-piece bathing suit while sunbathing on the back patio.

Kierra loved her sister, but she chose Oxford for a reason.

YOU'RE NOT ANYWHERE THAT I CAN'T FIND YOU

(AFTER PHIL COLLINS)

PHIL SLOWLY STIRRED in his bed as the phone rang. He glanced at the clock. It was nearly 2 AM. Late calls normally signaled an emergency, so he willed himself awake, sat on the edge of his bed, and answered the phone.

"It's me. Billy," said the voice on the other end.

"Billy who?"

"You told me to call you if I ever needed you."

Phil shook the remaining fog from his head. "Billy? It's you?"

"Yep. It's me. They're still chasing me. I don't know what to do."

"Shit. I thought we'd squashed this thing over 30 years ago."

PURPLE

HE'D WRITTEN multiple stories titled after the same color. It wasn't that the color was his favorite; he just thought it would be cool to play with the idea in different ways over the course of different pieces. He'd even considered naming the larger collection after the color, but it was a color more closely linked to another Artist's brand, not his own.

As he began to read the reviews of his book, many readers pointed out what they perceived as his obsession with the color.

For fun, he'd write another story with that title for his next book, too.

SOON I'LL BE LOVING YOU AGAIN

(AFTER MARVIN GAYE)

THAT SATURDAY MORNING Mama was folding clothes while humming along with Marvin Gaye.

"What does 'I wanna give you some head' mean?" I asked.

"What did you just say?" She stopped cold, giving me *the eye.*

"Marvin keeps saying it over and over."

"No, he doesn't."

"Listen to him, Mama."

She turned up the volume and leaned in closer to the speaker.

Her face turned white, and she promptly turned the record off.

Later that night when my father got home from work and showered, the two of them sat beside the speaker listening to Marvin, giggling softly to themselves.

ACKNOWLEDGMENTS

"The Other Side of (Madison)" and "Death and the Tsunami" were originally published in *The Drabble*. "Three Books" was originally published in *Story in 100 Words*. "Colorful" and "Dumas" were originally published in *The Dribble Drabble Review*. "Screamin' Sisyphus," The Gift," and "The Libraries" were originally published in *Friday Flash Fiction*. "Tears in the Fabric of Us," "The Comedian," "Absolution," "Numbers," "Eric's Things, Circa 1985," and "Fear" were originally published in *The Centifictionist*. "Posthumous" was originally published in *Fewer Than 500*. "Grandma's Photograph" was originally published in *Down in the Dirt Magazine*. "All White Male Authors Look Alike" was originally published in *100 Word Story*. "Apocalyptic Ambivalence" was originally published in *Free Flash Fiction*. "Buckroe" was originally published in *Microfiction Monday Magazine*. "Sauce" was originally published in *Can I Kick It: Sneaker Microfiction and Poetry*. "La traductora" was originally published in *Rue Scribe*.

∾

Special thanks to my wife and daughter, who make it possible for me to write, and to all of my family, friends, and colleagues who continue to support me and my work.

ALSO BY RAN WALKER

ABOUT THE AUTHOR

Ran Walker is the author of twenty-three books. He is the winner of the 2019 Indie Author of the Year and 2019 BCALA Fiction Ebook Awards. He teaches creative writing at Hampton University and lives with his wife and daughter in Virginia. He can be reached via his website, www.ranwalker.com.

CPSIA information can be obtained
at www.ICGtesting.com
Printed in the USA
BVHW040233100921
616508BV00017B/634